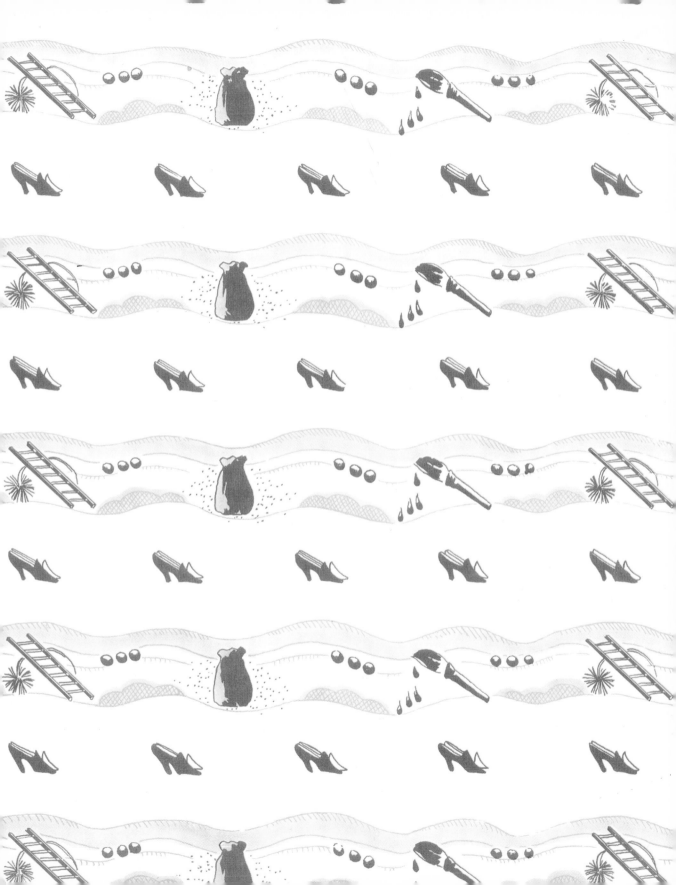

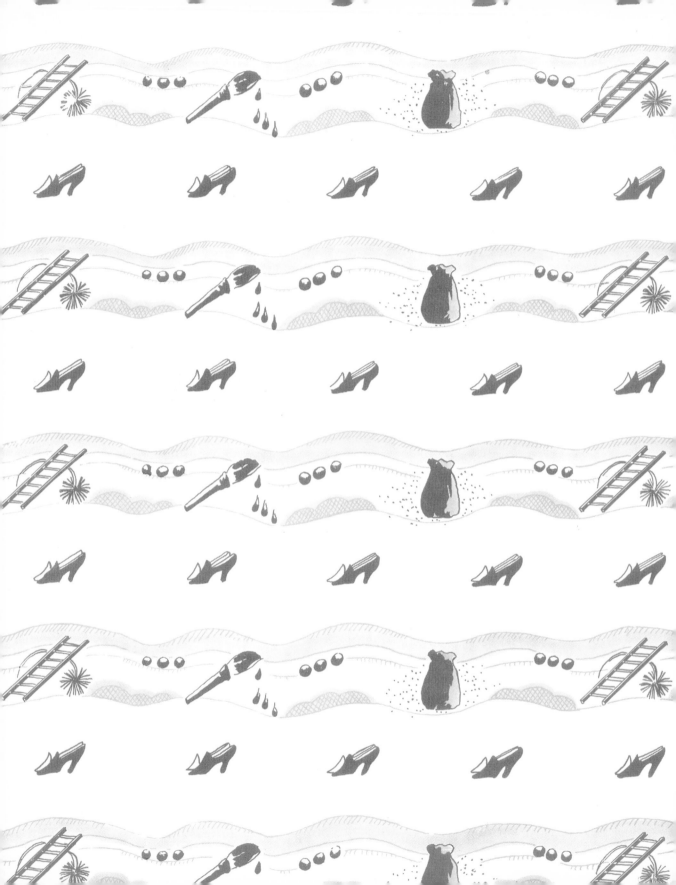

Snipp, Snapp, Snurr
and the
RED SHOES

MAJ LINDMAN

ALBERT WHITMAN & COMPANY
Morton Grove, Illinois

The Snipp, Snapp, Snurr Books
Snipp, Snapp, Snurr and the Red Shoes
Snipp, Snapp, Snurr and the Gingerbread
Snipp, Snapp, Snurr and the Buttered Bread (March 1995)
Snipp, Snapp, Snurr Learn to Swim (March 1995)

The Flicka, Ricka, Dicka Books
Flicka, Ricka, Dicka and the New Dotted Dresses
Flicka, Ricka, Dicka and the Three Kittens
Flicka, Ricka, Dicka Bake a Cake (March 1995)
Flicka, Ricka, Dicka and the Little Dog (March 1995)

ISBN 0-8075-7496-1
LC 94-13629

The text is set in 23' Futura Book
and 12' Bookman Light Italic.

A Snipp, Snapp, Snurr Book

"I would like a pair of red shoes, red shoes lined with gold."

Snipp, Snapp, and Snurr were three little boys who lived in Sweden. Their hair was yellow and their eyes were blue, and they looked very much alike.

One day Snipp said, "Mother dear, tomorrow will be your birthday. Snapp and Snurr and I have talked about it, but we can't decide what to get you for a birthday present."

Snipp said, "I thought you might like a train."

Snapp said, "I thought you might like a pony."

Snurr said, "I know! You would like to have a red wagon!"

Mother thought for a moment. Then she said, "I would like a pair of red shoes, red shoes lined with gold."

Snipp, Snapp, and Snurr decided that Mother must have her red shoes.

They ran upstairs to their playroom to get their bank, which was a white china pig with brown spots. The bank was on the high bookcase.

Snipp brought a chair.

Snapp climbed upon the chair, stood on tiptoe, reached for the bank, and handed it to Snurr. Then he climbed down.

The three little boys ran over to the table. They rattled their bank. They shook it and rolled it from side to side to try to get out all their money.

But as long and as hard as they shook, they could not get out enough money to buy the red shoes.

They rattled their bank.

Snipp, Snapp, and Snurr decided that they must find a way to earn money. The three little boys asked their mother if they might go out. When she said yes, they hurried outside and down the street. All three of them were looking for ways to earn money.

Near the corner light, they saw a neighbor painting a board fence. The fence was so high that the man had to stand on a wooden box to reach the top.

Snipp said politely, "Do you need help, sir? I am quite sure that I could finish painting that fence."

The neighbor had many other things to do, so he was glad to have Snipp finish the painting.

"Do you need help, sir?"

Snapp and Snurr walked on down the street. They were thinking of ways to earn money to buy those red shoes.

High on the roof of a house, they saw the village chimney sweep. He was cleaning out a chimney with brushes.

Suddenly he called loudly, "Snapp, come and help me!"

Both Snapp and Snurr climbed up a ladder and across the roof, to the tallest chimney.

The man was nearly as dirty as the chimney he was sweeping. He smiled kindly as he said, "Snapp, you are so little you can get into the chimney and sweep it cleaner than I can. I will pay you if you will help me."

The man was nearly as dirty as the chimney he was sweeping.

So Snurr left Snapp on the roof and climbed down all alone.

Snipp was painting a bright red fence.

Snapp was cleaning out the very dirtiest chimney he had ever seen.

Snurr walked on, wondering what he could find to do. He *must* earn money to help buy the red shoes!

At last, Snurr saw a big mill where wheat was ground into flour. Before the mill stood Snurr's friend the miller. He wore a bright red cap and was smoking his longest pipe.

Snurr stepped up to him and said, "Please, sir, will you give me a job?"

The miller laughed, "Well, well, Snurr, what do you say? You want to be a miller? Good! You can begin work now."

"Please, sir, will you give me a job?"

All three boys were very happy. Each one had found a way to earn money to help buy the red shoes for his mother.

Snipp busily drew his brush up and down the fence. He felt very important.

The fence grew brighter and brighter until it glistened in the sun.

Snipp worked so fast and used so much red paint that he spilled some of it on his clothes. He even splashed red paint on his cheeks and on his bare legs. So as the fence grew redder and redder, Snipp grew redder and redder, too.

Soon his suit, which was once such a pretty blue, was all splattered with red.

Snipp grew redder and redder.

Snapp's suit was not much better! Snapp pushed his brush up and down the dirty chimney. The soot flew all over his nose and his hair and his clothes. Soon his pretty blue suit was gray. Then it grew darker. And the longer he worked, the grayer he got.

But Snapp was glad. Soon bright coins would jingle in his pocket, and the coins would help to buy the red shoes for Mother.

So Snapp worked harder than ever, whistling a little tune.

The longer he worked, the grayer he got.

Snurr was working at the flour mill. Once he even surprised the miller by carrying a large sack of flour.

Snurr worked hard, and he grew white from head to foot. He looked just like a snowman.

Money jingled cheerily in Snurr's pockets as he left the mill. The miller had been much pleased with his work.

Snurr now had his share of the money to help buy red shoes for his mother.

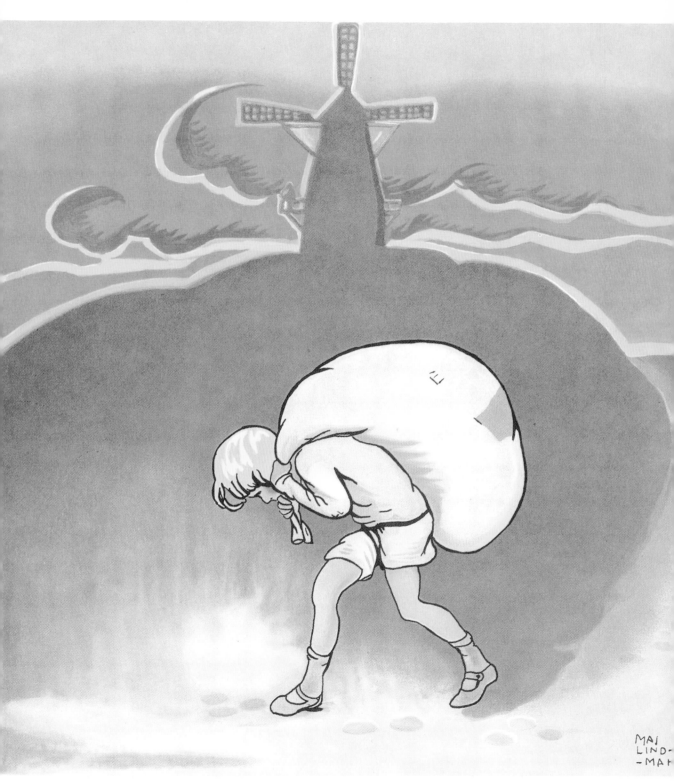

Snurr was working at the flour mill.

Snipp, Snapp, and Snurr all finished their work at the same time.

As they were running home, they met in the marketplace.

The little boy in red was Snipp.

The little boy in gray was Snapp.

The little boy in white was Snurr.

Each took his money out of his pocket.

When they counted all their money, they found that now they had enough to buy the red shoes.

Snipp, Snapp, and Snurr were very happy!

They decided to hurry to the shoemaker right away to see if he had the red shoes.

They counted all their money.

Down the street they ran. It was nearly sunset, and they were afraid the shop might close.

They dashed into the shoemaker's shop, each carrying his part of the money.

Because Snipp was in the lead, he began, "Mr. Shoemaker, have you—"

Because Snapp was next, he said, "Red shoes lined with gold?"

Because Snurr was last he finished, "Shoes that will fit our mother's feet?"

The shoemaker laughed. "Have I red shoes lined with gold that will fit your mother's feet? That I have. They are right here on the shelf. They are the finest you can buy, near or far."

"Shoes that will fit our mother's feet?"

Snipp, Snapp, and Snurr gave the shoemaker their money.

The shoemaker wrapped the shoes up in a box, and the three little boys hurried home, each taking a turn carrying the package.

At last they were home. Because Snipp was the first to find work, Snapp and Snurr agreed that he should be the one to give the package to Mother.

"Here is a present for you, Mother!" they cried as they burst into the door.

Mother was surprised to see a boy in red, a boy in gray, and a boy in white, instead of her three little boys in blue.

"Snipp, Snapp, and Snurr! Where have you been?" she cried.

"Here is a present for you, Mother!"

We have been earning money to buy you a birthday present, Mother dear, and here it is!" they answered.

Mother untied the string, unwrapped the box, and took out the red shoes lined with gold.

"Why, here are the red shoes that I wanted more than anything else," she cried. "They are the most beautiful shoes in the world!"

She was so happy that she waved her lovely red shoes in the air.

Snipp, Snapp, and Snurr joined hands and danced around and around their mother.

As they danced, they sang, "Happy birthday! Happy birthday!"

"Happy birthday! Happy birthday!"

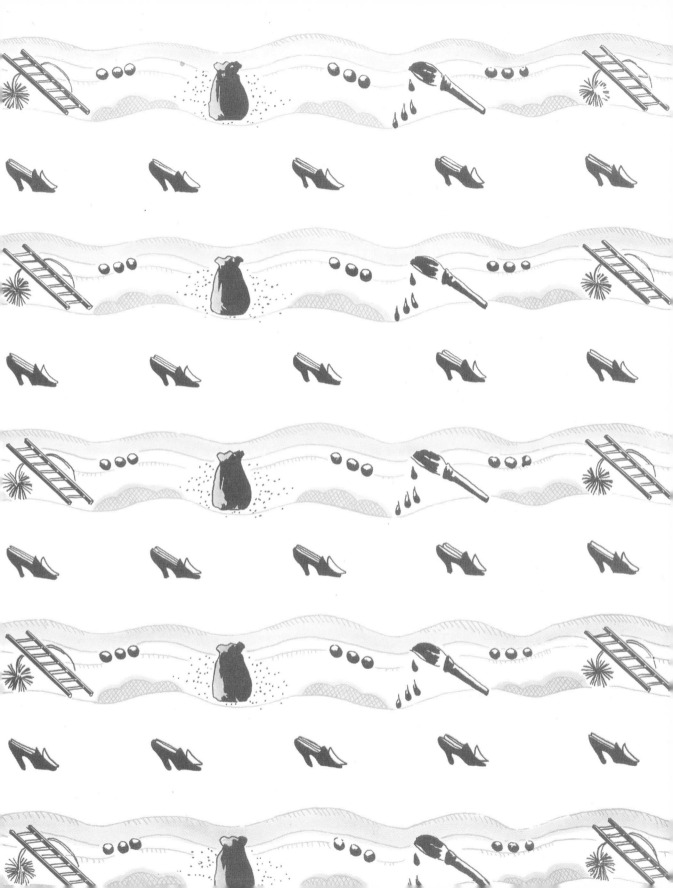

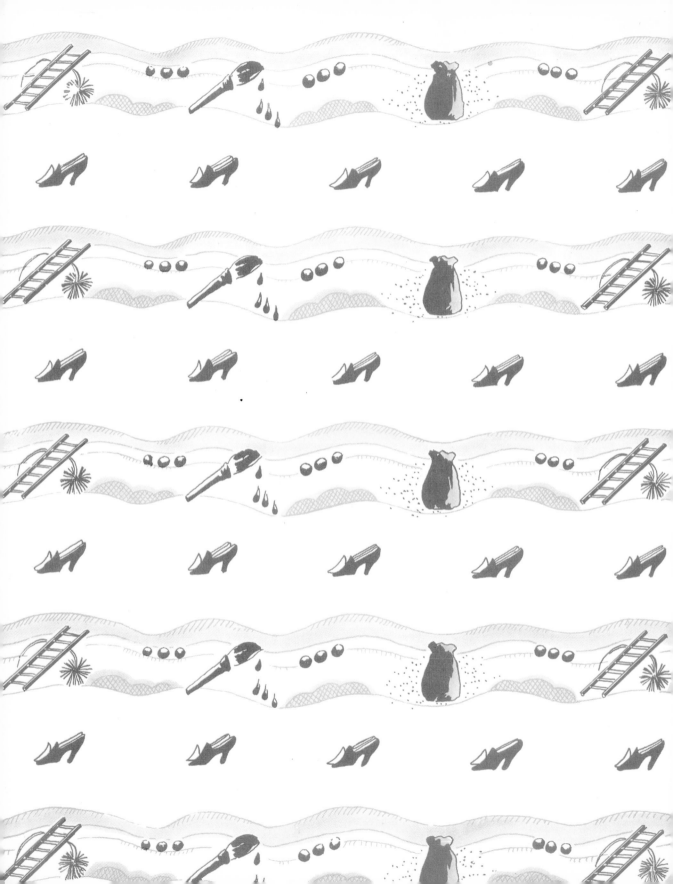